HAPPY BIRTHDAY

by James Young

S0-BYC-950

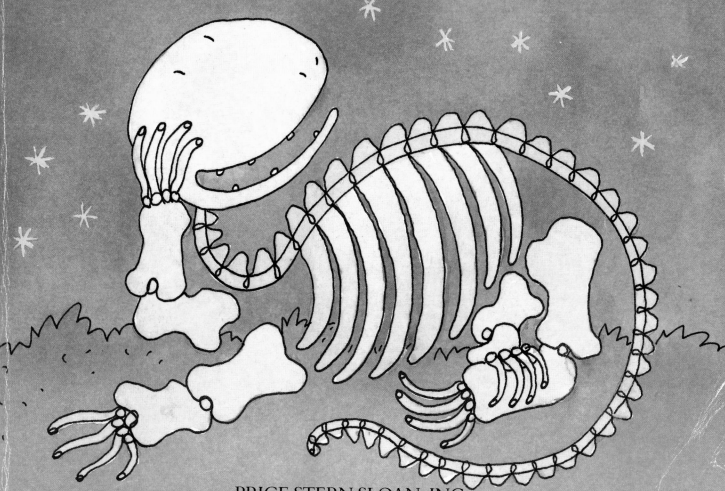

PRICE STERN SLOAN, INC.

Los Angeles

Library of Congress Cataloging-in-Publication Data

Young, James, 1956–
  Happy birthday, Og.

  Summary: Og the dinosaur feels badly that no one remembers his sixty-five
millionth birthday at the museum where he lives.
  [1. Dinosaurs—Fiction. 2. Birthdays—Fiction] I. Title.
PZ7.Y86518Hap 1987   [E]   87-30029
ISBN 0-8431-2223-4

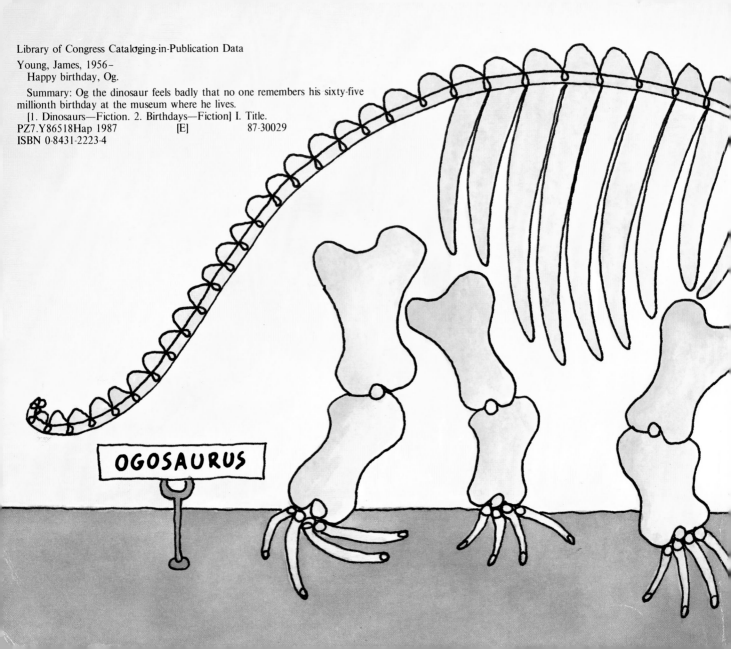

OGOSAURUS

Og lived in the Hall of Dinosaurs. He was sixty-five million years old and today was his birthday.

Copyright © 1987 by James Young
Published by Price Stern Sloan, Inc., 360 North La Cienega Boulevard, Los Angeles, California 90048

Printed in the United States of America. All rights reserved. No part of this publication may be reproduced, stored in a retrieval system or transmitted, in any form or by any means, electronic, mechanical photocopying, recording or otherwise, without the prior written permission of the publisher.

ISBN: 0-8431-2223-4

But no one remembered! Wendell, the museum guard, didn't remember.

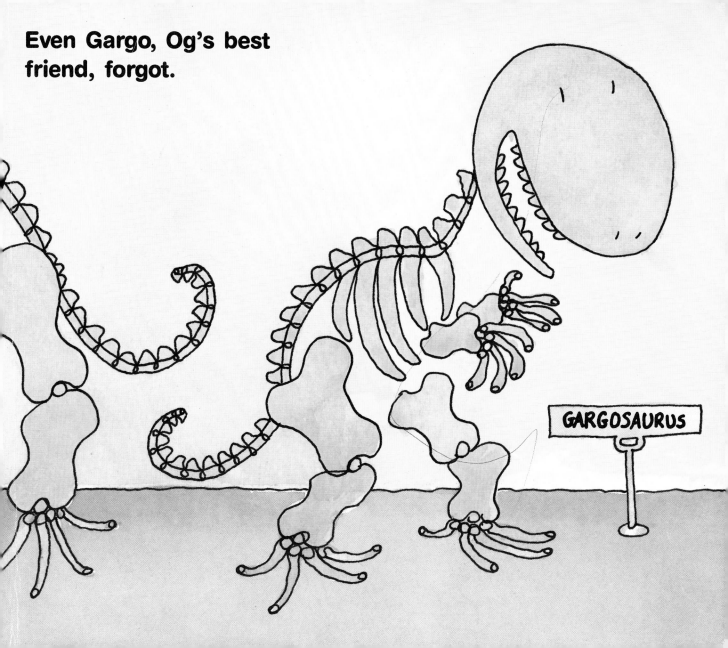

Even Gargo, Og's best friend, forgot.

GARGOSAURUS

All day long people came and looked at Og,
but no one wished him a happy birthday.

Finally Og said to himself, "Well, there must be someone somewhere who remembers my birthday."

He quietly crept through the dark halls of the museum. Only the old stuffed saber-toothed tiger saw him go by.

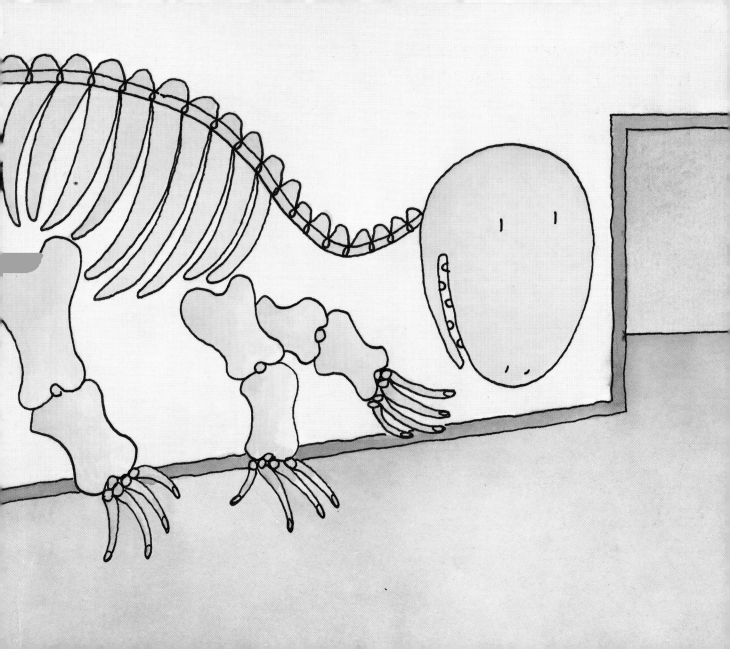

Slowly, he squeezed through the giant
doors of the museum and he was outside.

But nothing was the way he remembered it.

The streets were full of people, all going places. Not one of them wished him a happy birthday.

Cars beeped and honked at him. No one had time to stop for Og.

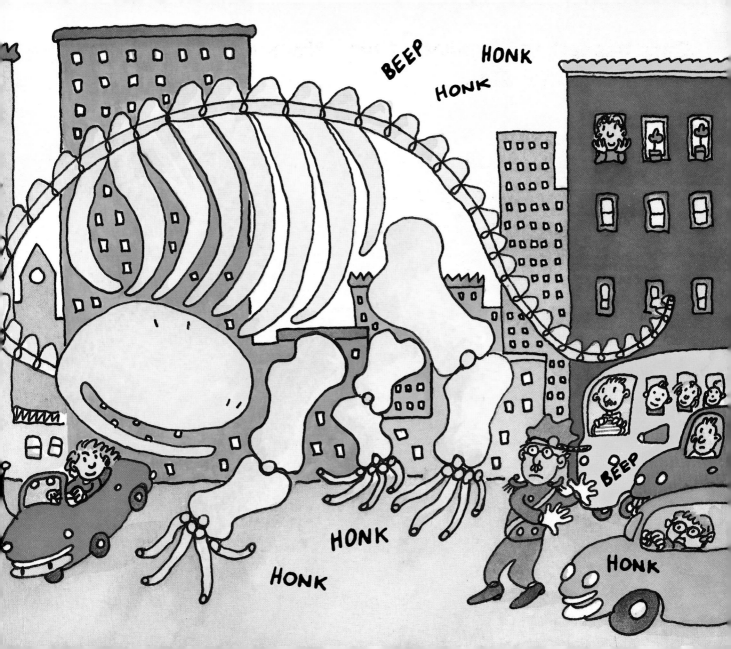

Everything was bigger and louder and
faster than he had ever imagined.

When it got dark, the stars came out. At least they hadn't changed. They were almost the way he remembered them. "I'm glad the stars are still here," Og thought to himself.

The stars were old, even older than Og. He looked
at them for a long time. "I guess no one ever says
'Happy Birthday' to them either. Happy Birthday, Stars,"
he said and then Og went home—

**back up the stairs of the museum
and through the giant doors.**

But it was dark in the Hall of Dinosaurs. "Everyone must be asleep," Og said to himself. "I'll have to be very quiet." When suddenly—

It was the best birthday Og could remember. And he blew out all the candles by himself, all sixty-five million of them!